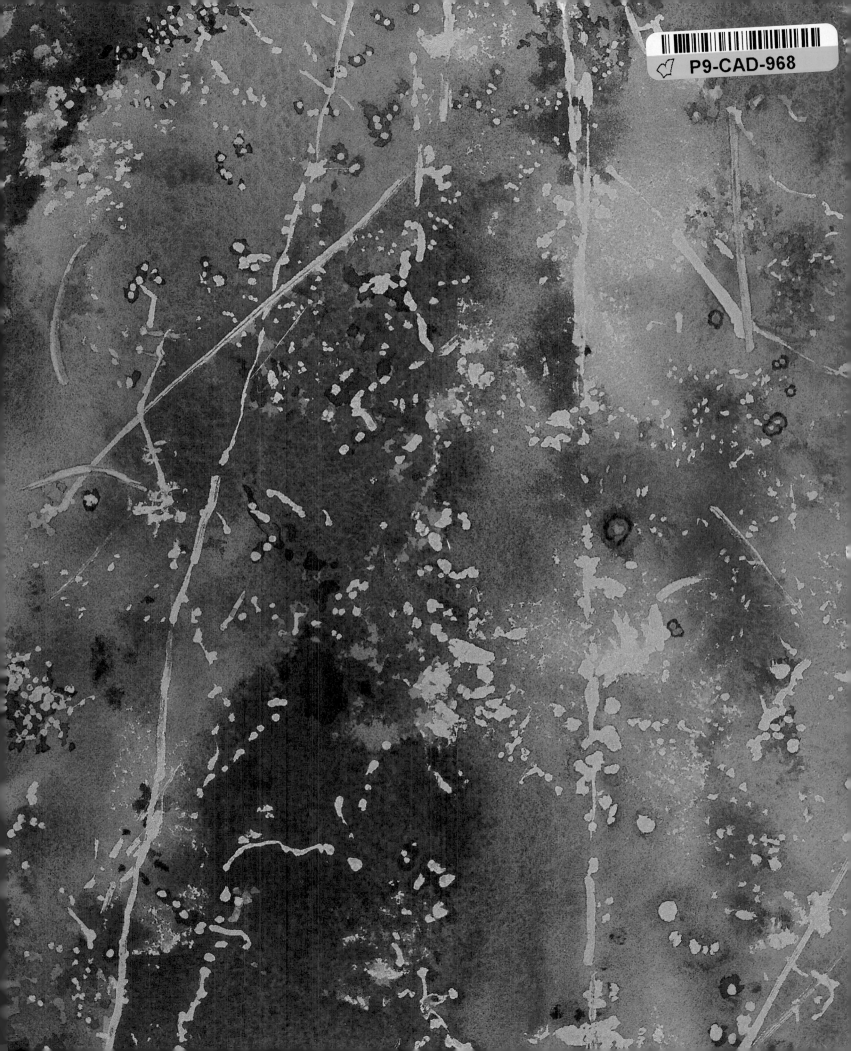
P9-CAD-968

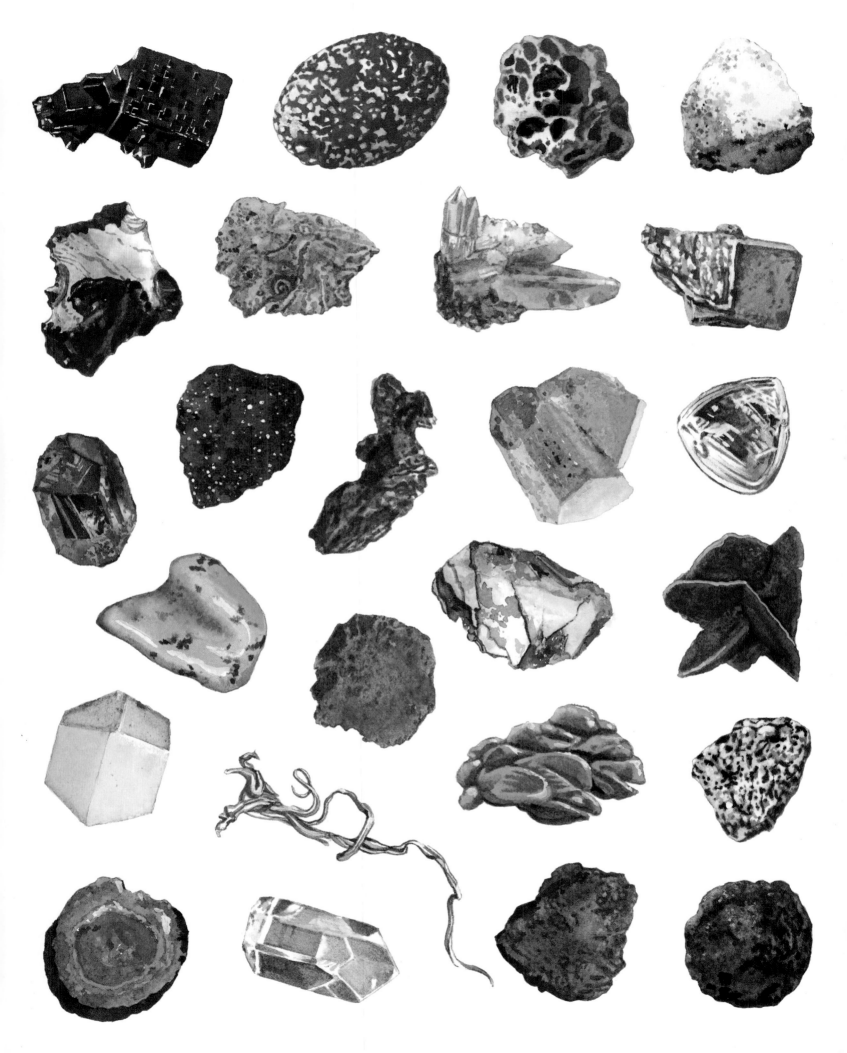

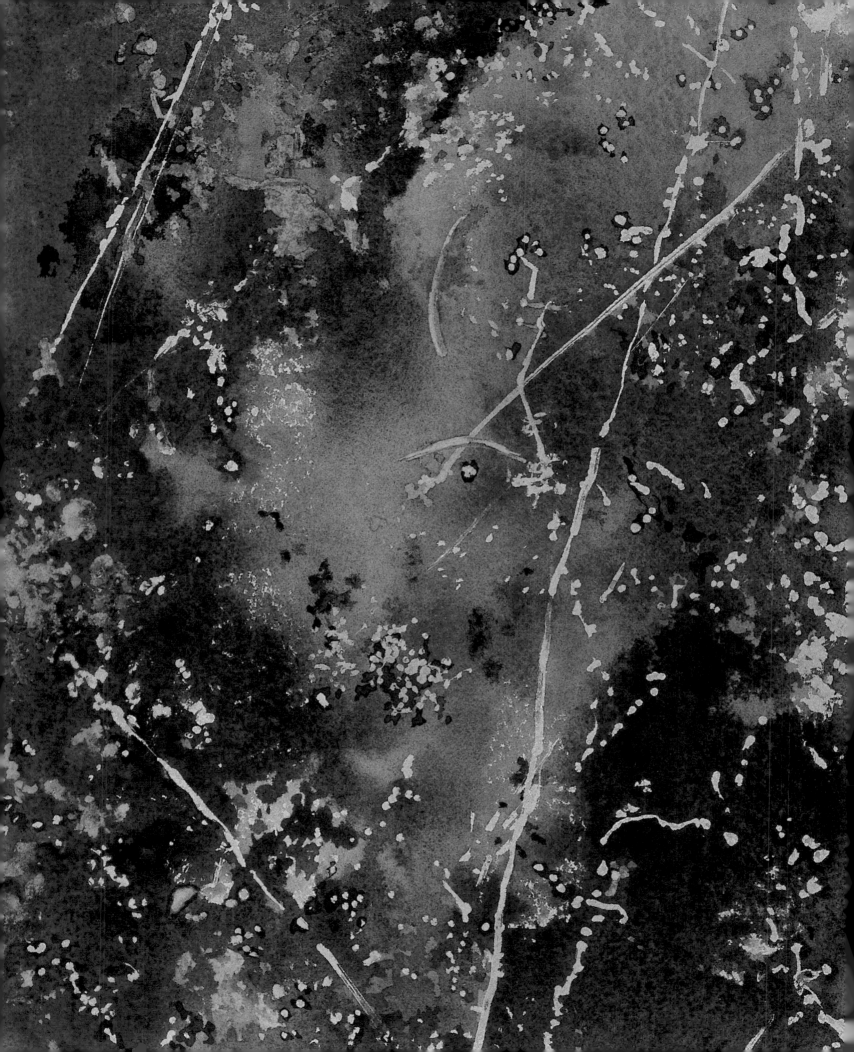

A Rock Is Lively

Azurite Geode

Granite

Chrysocolla

Sandstone

To Fox Carmody —D. H. A.

To Thomas Lyman Carlisle, MD, my genius brother,
who had *the* coolest rock collection when we were kids. —S. L.

ACKNOWLEDGMENTS:

My father, Frank J. Carlisle, Jr., whose lifelong fascination with geology
resulted in many lectures about basin and range country, alluvial fans,
dikes, and scarp and dip slopes as we drove across the country
for childhood summer vacations.

Edward Garnero, Phd., Professor, School of Earth and Space Exploration, Arizona State University, Tempe, AZ.
Craig Daniel, (virtual) Lehigh Valley Museum of Natural History, Allentown, PA.
Candace A. Sall, Associate Curator, Museum of Anthropology, University of Missouri, Columbus, Missouri.
Robert Spomer, Buena Vista Gem Works.
Rob Lavinsky, iRocks.com

Text © 2012 by Dianna Hutts Aston.
Illustrations © 2012 by Sylvia Long.
All rights reserved. No part of this book may be reproduced
in any form without written permission from the publisher.

Library of Congress Cataloging-in-Publication Data

Aston, Dianna Hutts.
A rock is lively / Dianna Hutts Aston, Sylvia Long.
p. cm.
ISBN 978-1-4521-0645-8 (alk. paper)
1. Rocks—Juvenile literature. 2. Minerals—Juvenile literature. I. Long, Sylvia. II. Title.
QE432.2.A88 2012
552—dc23
2011048375

Book design by Sara Gillingham.
Hand lettered by Anne Robin and Sylvia Long.
The illustrations in this book were rendered in watercolor.

Manufactured in China.

7 9 10 8

Chronicle Books LLC
680 Second Street, San Francisco, California 94107
www.chroniclekids.com

Fairburn Agate

Fairburn Agate

Silver

A Rock Is Lively

Dianna Hutts Aston + Sylvia Long

chronicle books · san francisco

Whiting Public Library
Whiting, Indiana

A rock is lively . . .

Snowflake Obsidian

...bubbling like a pot of soup
deep beneath the earth's crust...
liquid...molten...boiling.

Depending on what type of rock it is,
a rock melts at temperatures between
1,300 and 2,400 degrees Fahrenheit
(700 and 1,300 degrees Celsius).

A rock is mixed up.

All rocks are made of a mix of ingredients called minerals. Just as a batter of flour, butter, and sugar makes a cookie, a batter of minerals makes a rock. The recipe for a rock might include minerals like aluminum, copper, diamond, fluorite, gold, gypsum, lead, nickel, platinum, quartz, silver, sulfur, tin, topaz, and turquoise.

Sodalite

Calcite

Pyrite

Lazurite

Lapis Lazuli

Mix the mineral lazurite with a
dash of sodalite and a pinch of
both calcite and pyrite Heat within
the earth until a brilliant blue.

Lapis Lazuli

A rock is galactic

Outer space is a shower of rocky fireworks

Asteroid

Meteoroid

METEOROIDS are rocks that range in size from a grain of sand to a basketball. They become meteors or "shooting stars," when they streak through Earth's atmosphere and vaporize. Sometimes pieces of the meteor aren't vaporized and land on Earth's surface. These are called meteorites.

COMETS are balls of rock and ice—sometimes called "dirty snowballs"—that are heated by the sun and soar through space, leaving glowing ribbons of dust behind them.

Comet

ASTEROIDS are gigantic chunks of rocks and metal. They can weigh millions of tons. The largest known asteroid is 650 miles (1,050 kilometers) in diameter. It would take a person 352 hours, or nearly 15 days, to walk around it.

A rock is old.

The oldest known rocks on Earth were formed billions of years before the sky turned from green to blue, before dinosaurs thundered across the earth, before humans learned how to make fire. The oldest rocks ever found are nearly 4.5 billion years old.

METEORITE FRAGMENT
Algeria,
4.4 billion years old

GREENSTONE
Canada,
4.28 billion years old

ZIRCON CRYSTAL
Australia,
4.1 billion years old

LEWISIAN GNEISS
Scotland,
3 billion years old

GRANITE
United States,
2.5 billion years old

A rock is huge...

Considered by many to be the world's largest rock, Australia's
Mount Augustus is a sandstone rock with an *elevation*, or height,
of 3,628 feet (1,106 meters) above sea level—about 1,000 feet (305 meters)
higher than the world's tallest skyscraper.

or tiny.

The carpets of sand on the floors and shores of oceans, lakes, and rivers come from larger rocks that have been ground, through weathering, into tiny grains.

A rock

Some birds swallow stones to help them digest food. As the muscles in the gizzards of their stomachs move, food is "chewed"—crushed by rocks in the same way humans use teeth to break down food.

Crocodiles, seals, and sea lions also ingest rocks. The extra weight, or *ballast*, helps them dive deeper and stay steady in water.

is helpful.

Sea otters lie on their backs and use rocks to crack open shells on their stomachs. Seagulls drop mollusks onto rocks to break apart their shells.

Chimpanzees and crows crack the hard shells of nuts on rocks.

Amethyst Geode

Laguna Agate

A rock is surprising.

Idar-Oberstein Agate

Blue Lace Agate

Malachite and Azurite Geode

Septarian Geode

Azurite Geode

Some rocks need to be broken open to reveal their beauty. Geodes—round, hollow rocks found mostly in deserts or beds of volcanic ash—hide sparkly crystals. The crystals were once liquids but, trapped inside rock for thousands of years, they changed into "jewels" of many colors.

Agates, too, with their colorful layers created by liquid deposits, are often found in volcanic rock.

Watermelon Tourmaline

Chrysanthemum Rock

A rock is inventive.

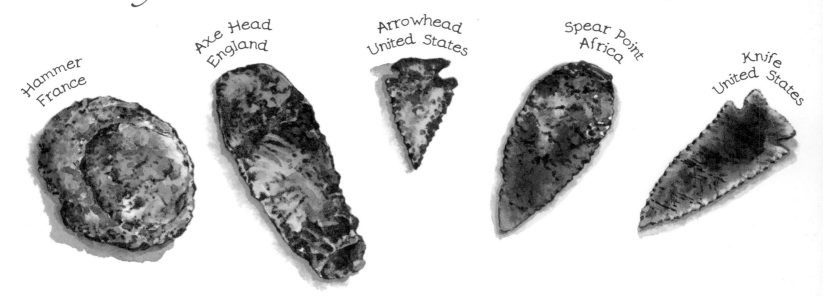

Hammer
France

Axe Head
England

Arrowhead
United States

Spear Point
Africa

Knife
United States

Long ago, humans chiseled rocks into sharp-edged weapons
and tools. Flaky flint and obsidian rocks were chipped into
arrowheads, spear points, axes, and hammers. Rough granite,
sandstone, and lava rocks were shaped into mortars and pestles
used for grinding seeds, rice, nuts, chiles, and garlic into food.

Mortar & Pestle, Greece

Today, humans use rocks to make cement and bricks, paper and pencils, glass, and toothpaste.

Quartz

Graphite

Limestone

Chalk

Limonite

Hematite

Limonite

Hematite

Manganese

A rock is creative.

Tens of thousands of years ago, before there was writing, ancient peoples
told stories through symbols. With colors made from minerals,
they painted pictographs on cave walls, rock shelters, and ledges.
They chipped and pecked the surface of stones to make petroglyphs.

Pictograph — Lascaux, France, 12,000 to 17,000 years old

Petroglyph — Nine Mile Canyon, Utah, 1,000 years old

Limestone — Pyramids of Giza, Egypt,
4,100 to 4,600 years old

Basalt and other volcanic rocks —
Moai, Easter Island,
500 to 750 years old

In more recent history, artists and builders have chiseled great sculptures and monuments from all kinds of rock.

Sandstone, dolerite, and others — Stonehenge, England, 3,100 to 5,100 years old

Marble — Taj Mahal, India,
about 400 years old

Onyx — "Mother and Child" by
Isamu Noguchi, United States,
about 60 years old

Marble — "David" by
Michelangelo, Italy,
about 500 years old

Granite — Mt. Rushmore, United States, almost 100 years old

A rock is recycled.

SEDIMENTARY rocks, like coal and lime-stone, have eroded over time into smaller pieces of sand, pebbles, and gravel, then were pressed together like a layer cake with fossils, seashells, and decayed plants.

METAMORPHIC rocks began as sedimentary or igneous, but were baked and squeezed so hard by heat and pressure, they became metamorphic rocks like slate and marble.

IGNEOUS rocks are formed by magma. When magma erupts through volcanoes, it cools and hardens into rocks like granite and pumice. Pumice is so lightweight, it floats!

A rock doesn't hurry. Over thousands of millions of years, it changes from one form to another. This is called the rock cycle. In a process called *erosion*, a rock is squashed and scraped by glaciers, whirled by waves and rain, and pushed deep into the earth until it turns into magma.

Then a rock is once again...

lively!

obsidian

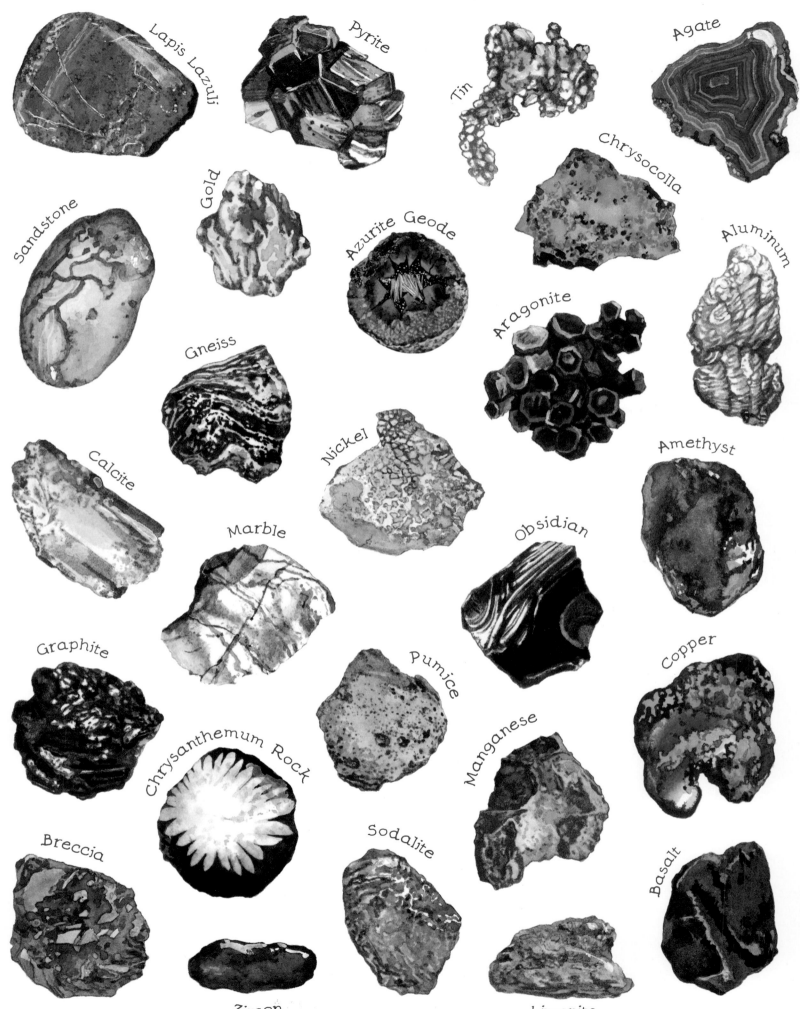

Lapis Lazuli

Pyrite

Tin

Agate

Chrysocolla

Sandstone

Gold

Azurite Geode

Aluminum

Aragonite

Gneiss

Nickel

Amethyst

Calcite

Marble

Obsidian

Graphite

Pumice

Copper

Chrysanthemum Rock

Manganese

Breccia

Sodalite

Basalt

Zircon

Limonite

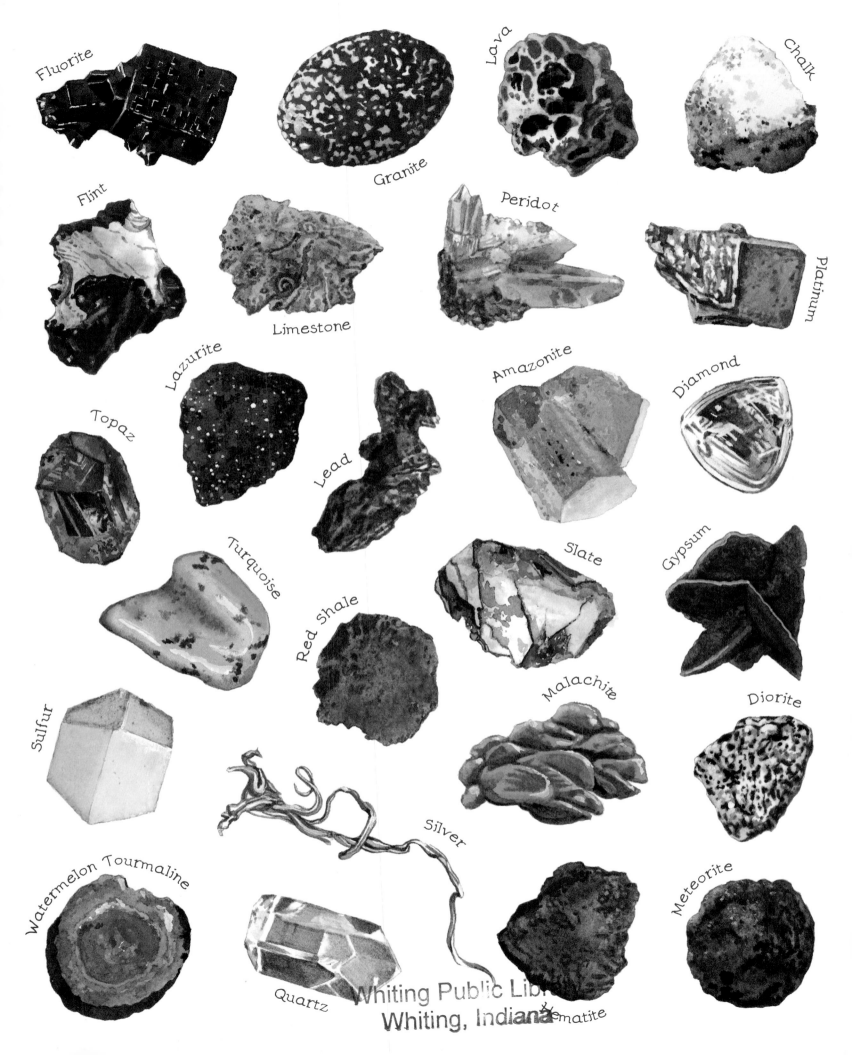

Fluorite

Granite

Lava

Chalk

Flint

Limestone

Peridot

Platinum

Lazurite

Topaz

Lead

Amazonite

Diamond

Turquoise

Red Shale

Slate

Gypsum

Sulfur

Malachite

Diorite

Silver

Watermelon Tourmaline

Quartz

Hematite

Meteorite

Whiting Public Library
Whiting, Indiana